Emily & the Captain:
A High Seas Adventure

By Noelle Hall
Illustrated by Mel D'Souza

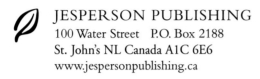

JESPERSON PUBLISHING
100 Water Street   P.O. Box 2188
St. John's NL Canada A1C 6E6
www.jespersonpublishing.ca

Library and Archives Canada Cataloguing in Publication

Hall, Noelle, 1957–

Emily & the Captain : A High Seas Adventure / by Noelle Hall; Illustrated by Mel D'Souza.

For ages 8-12.

ISBN 1-894377-15-X
I. D'Souza, Mel II. Title. III. Title: Emily and the Captain.

PS3515.A364E46 2005   j813'.6   C2005-902147-0

Printed and bound by Replika Press Pvt. Ltd., India.

Dedication

To all my friends who are too numerous to mention.
Especially to those that appreciate the uniqueness in us all.
And for those that share my love and desire for Newfoundland.
One day, we will go *home* never to leave and then we will feel our
souls flying free as we embrace and dance along the rocky shores.

1 Fear Sets In

Emily was worried. So very worried. She, Ann and Betty stood out by the lighthouse staring towards the mouth of the bay hoping to catch sight of Captain Woody and the crew of the *Georgia K*. The ship was late. Very late indeed.

In June, Emily had freed Captain Woodrow McKenzie, who everyone called Captain Woody, from the spell of the evil wicked Santana, the sea imp, which had kept the Captain locked deep within the walls of the lighthouse for a very long time. Emily and Captain Woody had been married and were looking forward to their future together. But now, the Captain was late returning and Emily was so afraid something terrible had happened. There had been no word from the *Georgia K*.

Captain Woody and his crew had sailed from Woody Point over a month ago to drop off and pick up cargo in Labrador. From there they were headed to St. John's to make a delivery and load cargo bound for Woody Point. The *Georgia K* was to bring back important items that the

local merchants and residents had ordered. If the Captain did not get back, a lot of residents would be short of much-needed winter supplies.

Emily had been going out by the lighthouse every day hoping to see the ship sailing into the bay. Sometimes wives of the crewmembers would join her. As each day passed, they became more worried and fearful. They would gladly exchange all the goods in the world to have their loved ones back home. What was wrong? Why were they not back yet?

2 Aboard the *Georgia K*

The trip to Labrador had been uneventful. The ship had unloaded and loaded cargo in record time. From there, Captain Woody and his crew had smooth sailing all the way to St. John's. Their spirits were high. If the weather held, the men would be home in lots of time to finish preparing for winter.

The *Georgia K* docked in St. John's harbour. While the cargo was being unloaded, Captain Woody and several of his crew strolled down Water Street visiting the local merchants and filling orders for the people back home. Once the parcels were added to the cargo hold, the ship sailed out of the harbour and through the narrows. A calm sea and a gentle breeze greeted the *Georgia K*. The crew felt this was the sign of a quick trip home.

Late on the second day, their luck changed. The skies darkened and the winds picked up. Before they knew it, the waves were tossing the ship about. The battle against the angry seas continued for hours. The men grew weary and exhausted from their struggle.

At last the wind died and the sea calmed. Feeling safe and relieved, the crew

started to assess the damage to the vessel. Captain Woody went to the bridge to see how far they had been blown off course. He had just bent over his desk to study the charts when Charlie, his first mate, bellowed in fright. The Captain ran out to see what was wrong. The deck hands were all shouting and pointing over the starboard bow.

Heading directly towards them was a huge waterspout. Before Captain Woody could issue any orders, the swiftly spinning waterspout picked up the *Georgia K* and held the ship within its grasp. Everyone aboard was helpless and desperately trying to hang on so they would not be flung out of the vessel. The *Georgia K* kept whirling and spinning until finally, the waterspout stopped and dropped the ship slamming it into the water.

When the Captain came to his senses, the first thing he heard was someone laughing. This was very puzzling. How could anyone find humour in this horrible situation? He glared over in the direction of the hideous laughter.

"You! No, it can't be! This can not be real. I destroyed you along time ago," said the astonished Captain.

Santana, the evil wicked sea imp, was standing on the deck ripping apart the ship's radio and flinging the pieces into the sea. He took the antenna, bent it and broke it across his leg and let those pieces fall into the sea also.

"Yes, Captain, you thought you destroyed me, but you only wounded me. It took a long time for my wounds to mend. During this time, my spies filled me in on what was going on in Woody Point. When I heard how that meddling northern light helped you and then Emily's love finally freed you, I vowed your happiness would be short lived."

As Santana started to lunge towards Captain Woody, Charlie, who had snuck up behind him, jumped on the evil creature pinning him to the deck. The Captain helped Charlie tie up the squirming imp and they hauled him over to the side of the ship. Several crewmembers joined in to help throw Santana overboard. One of the men even tied an anchor to the miserable creature, in the hopes that he would never resurface again.

As Santana was being thrown overboard, he shouted, "It's not that easy, Captain! And now, I curse you and your crew. This ship will disappear, never to be found by mankind again. You will be stranded here forever!"

With a bone-chilling laugh, he sank into the sea.

Just then, a huge wave appeared out of nowhere. It picked up the *Georgia K* sending it hurtling towards the shore. When the water receded, the ship was beached on the shore of a small cove.

Captain Woody ordered the crew to get the lifeboats lowered onto the beach. They would at least be able to row to another community and find a way to come back and save the *Georgia K*. The lifeboats were lowered and the whole crew attempted to haul them into the water. But no matter how hard they pulled and tugged, the lifeboats would not budge. It was as if some unseen force was pulling against them. That unseen force was Santana's curse. When this dawned on the Captain, he ordered the crew to stop. It was of no use. Santana's curse was not to be broken that easily. Feelings of doom descended on the crew.

3 A Shoulder to Cry On

Emily heard a knock on the door. She rushed over and flung it wide, hoping it was someone with good news.

"Oh, it is only you," she said sadly.

"Well that is a fine way to greet a friend, I must say. Doesn't make me feel very welcome. Do you feel welcomed?" said John Lawrence, the moose, to his mate, Mildred.

The moose stood on Emily's front porch shaking their heads. Mildred the Moose stepped closer to Emily. "Gee Emily, have we done something to make you angry? I know we haven't been down to visit lately, but we figured you and the Captain were busy settling into your new home and new life as husband and wife."

Emily with tears in her eyes threw her arms around Mildred. "I am so sorry. I didn't mean to sound like I was unhappy to see you. You know how much I adore the two of you. It's just that I thought you might be

someone with news about Captain Woody. You see, his ship is missing and no one has heard anything! The coast guard has been searching and there has been no radio contact with them. It is as if the ship and all the crew has disappeared."

"You poor dear! Oh Emily, please try not to cry. You are making me cry too!" Mildred the Moose sniffed and moved her head slowly back and forth as she wiped her eyes on Emily's shoulders. "And look, even John Lawrence has tears in his eyes."

"I do not! I think it is pine needles. Humph, you know bull moose don't cry," said John Lawrence with a frown.

"Here," said Emily, "let me take a look." She peered into his eye and looked over at Mildred and winked. "Well yes, that is exactly what it is. Wait here, I'll go get some water to wash it out."

As Emily went into the house she heard John Lawrence, who was, after all, a very proud bull moose, tell Mildred, "See I told you. No way was I crying. Humph!"

As Emily was rinsing out his eye, she told them from the beginning about the missing Captain and his crew and how no one could find them. Mildred suggested that they get Leah the Eagle to fly out and search for the *Georgia K.*

"With those sharp eyes she can find anything."

"That is an excellent idea! Hey, we could get Toni the Trout to swim around and search too," added John Lawrence.

They all thought this was a grand idea and after the three friends munched on some apples, the moose headed back up to the Mystical Forest to find Leah the Eagle.

Leah the Eagle was perched up in a tree when they came around a bend. "Hello! Why are you two is such a hurry? Where are you going?"

"We were looking for you, Leah. You have just got to help Emily find Captain Woody." And so, the two moose told the eagle all about the lost ship. Leah agreed to talk to Toni the Trout so they could start searching for the Captain right away. She promised to return as soon as she could. Then, she soared out over the bay to go find Toni.

4 The Search is On

Toni the Trout spent her fall and winter in the deeper water near Lobster Cove Head lighthouse. She was dozing when she felt something hit her fin. There it was again. Pebbles were bouncing off her back and landing in her nice bed of kelp. Who would be messing up her place like this? She was very angry as she swam to the surface of the water. Just as she surfaced, a pebble hit her right on the head.

"Ouch! Leah, how dare you! You have not only dropped pebbles all over my nice clean home, but now you have hit me right on the head. Ouch, I say. Whatever has possessed you?"

"Lighten up Toni, get the broom and sweep the mess up. We have got bigger fish to fry, so to speak."

"Fish to fry! I don't like the sound of that! If you came here to insult me…"

"Now listen, Toni, the Captain and his ship are missing. No one can find them. It is up to us to go out and search."

Toni, still a little upset about the pebbles, mumbled and swam around awhile before answering. "Of course I will help. And you are right, pebbles can be swept away, but friends shouldn't be. Let's get going!"

Just as the search began for the *Georgia K*, thick fog rolled in and blocked their vision. Leah had a couple of near misses with some trees and Toni almost ran into a boat. How would they ever find the Captain in this fog? Leah was getting ready to stop the search for the night when she thought she saw a beam of light piercing its way through the thick fog. She stared at the light. It was getting brighter and bigger! Suddenly Glow-ria, the Northern Light was right in front of her.

"Glow-ria, what a welcome sight you are! Did you come to help us search for the Captain?"

"Yes, my dear friend, I am here to help," Glow-ria replied as she shimmered and shook. "I was in the Mystical Forest visiting Gregory A. Bear and Rhett the Fox, when I heard all about the search for Captain Woody. Let's all go down by those rocks so we can talk."

Glow-ria shrank and was soon resting beside the eagle on a rock with the trout in the shallow water below them.

"I have a strange feeling that Santana the evil sea imp is somehow the cause of this tragedy," Glow-ria said.

"But the Captain destroyed him a long time ago. How could he have anything to do with this? That would be horrible," gulped Toni.

"Yes, Glow-ria, whatever makes you think that? My feathers get all ruffled at just the thought of that evil creature!" Leah said as she tried to smooth her feathers back down.

"I have heard rumours about some strange and unusual things. I have even heard about sightings of an ugly looking creature that sounds just like Santana. I wish I had told Captain Woody about this before he sailed so he would be on the look out. But we can't dwell on that now. We must try to find the *Georgia K*," Glow-ria said.

With Glow-ria to help light the way in the thick fog, the group agreed to resume their search. To Toni's delight, Glow-ria suddenly got really big and bright and whistled. Magically more northern lights appeared in the sky. Some guided the trout through the rough water, while Glow-ria and several other lights flew with the eagle.

5 Mummers in the Night

Deep in the Mystical Forest, the animals gathered. They were very worried about the missing Captain. And they didn't like seeing Emily so upset.

"We need to do something to take Emily's mind off of things for awhile," said Gregory A. Bear, who, unlike most bears, never started hibernating until after New Year's.

"If only we could bring some merriment into her life. Make her smile. I really missed not seeing her smile the other day," John Lawrence the Moose said.

"Merriment you say?" asked Charlene the Caribou. "Let me tell you about something I saw last Christmas that might work. One night, I couldn't sleep so I wandered down towards the town and stood behind some alders looking at the lights on all the houses. While I was enjoying the scene, I heard music and laughter coming from Emily's friend, Ida's house. Curiosity took over so I crept up closer and looked in the window…" Charlene the Caribou continued her story about what she had seen that night. Her friends the animals all stood around amazed. When she finished her tale, everyone knew just what to do to cheer Emily up. With much giggling and snickering, the plan was set in motion. Then, they all scurried off to gather what they needed. Everyone would meet behind the lodge at eight o'clock that night.

Later that evening, Betty showed up at Emily's door with some pie. Ann arrived shortly after with cookies in hand. Emily put the kettle on so they could have tea. The three friends were sitting down to enjoy their snack when there was a loud knock on the door. Emily rushed over and swiftly pulled it open.

She screamed and slammed the door. "Thieves! There are thieves at my door!"

"Oh don't be so foolish, Emily, there are no thieves at that door." Betty shook her head and calmly drank her tea.

"Yes there are. They even have sheets and pillowcases over their heads so I won't know who they are. It's too late for Halloween, so it has to be thieves."

Ann put her cup down and smiled, "Sheets you say? Well, well, Emily that sounds like mummers to me, even though they are a little early. After all, this is only November."

"Mummers? What in the blazes are mummers?"

Betty got up from the table and headed to the door. "During Christmas, mummers are people dressed up in disguises. It is a very old custom. Once they are invited into a house, the mummers keep silent or disguise their voices when they talk. You have to guess who they are. You also have to give them a snack. They play a little music and everyone has a dance or two. Emily you must meet these mummers. Don't you agree, Ann?"

With that, Betty opened the door and saw that the mummers were walking away. She shouted for them to come back. As they got closer, with a big grin Betty turned to Ann and Emily, "Oh my word, these are not your typical mummers. Wait 'til you see this!"

The first mummer that strolled through the door was Rhett the Fox, plucking a beat up fiddle that only had one string. He was dressed in a flannel nightgown and had a shawl wrapped over his head. Only his sharp nose and beady eyes could be seen.

Next, in came John Lawrence the Moose dressed in foul weather gear. He had on yellow bibs with the suspenders attached to his antlers. A raincoat was snapped over his head. One eye was peeking out through. A sou'wester was perched on one of his antlers.

Mildred the Moose followed dressed in a big floral dress with a straw hat perched on top of the sheet that was covering her head.

Standing beside her was Charlene the Caribou in a one-piece long-john suit with the trap door flapping open. A burlap bag covered her head.

Last, but not least, was Gregory A. Bear standing there in rubber boots, a flannel shirt and bib overalls. A woollen ski mask covered his face. Gregory A. Bear bowed and then took Emily by the hand. As Rhett attempted to play his one-stringed fiddle, they had a little dance in the crowded living room. Betty tapped her feet to the music, while Ann picked up the Captain's accordion. The other animals swayed to the music. Emily's eyes were alive with laughter.

When the music stopped, Betty who had been eyeing the bear's flannel shirt looked at Emily, "So that is where that shirt went. I went to get it off the line this evening and it was gone. And Ida had told me one of Katie's gowns was missing. This explains everything."

"Uncle Howard told me one of his foul weather suits had gone missing from his fishing shed. Are those his rubber boots too? No one would ever believe this," Ann said in between fits of laughter.

Betty and Ann had seen through the animals' disguises. They could not communicate with them like Emily could, but greatly appreciated their surprise. Gregory A. Bear was so pleased he even went up and held out his paws to Emily's friends. The three of them danced a wonderful jig.

Emily served apples to the moose and the caribou. She opened a jar of jam for Gregory A. Bear. She presented Rhett the Fox with a peanut butter and jelly sandwich. Once they finished their snacks, Emily helped the animals out of their costumes. Ann agreed to help sneak some of the items back to Uncle Howard's shed. Betty took the flannel shirt and Katie's nightgown. The other costumes had been salvaged from the dump so they would not be missed by anyone.

Ann, who had walked with Emily to the end of the lane with the animals, listened as Emily spoke with them. She could not understand what the creatures were saying to Emily, but the love between the girl and her furry friends was obvious.

"All of you were great. What a grand surprise! I know you were trying to help take my mind off of things for a while, and you did. But I am still very worried," Emily sighed.

"Captain Woody will return. He will, Emily. With Glow-ria helping Leah and Toni he will be found. And then we can come down from the forest and mummer for him," Rhett the Fox said as he hugged Emily.

"Yes, dear Emily, you must keep the faith. The Captain will be home soon. You must believe in that," Mildred said as she sidled up next to Emily.

The animals all bid her farewell and made her promise to come to the forest for a toboggan ride once there was enough snow on the ground. They trotted up the road as Emily and Ann went down to their uncle's shed to return his belongings.

Emily felt so lucky to be surrounded by such wonderful friends–friends on two legs and friends on four.

6　New Recruits

Throughout the night and the next day, the search party continued to hunt for the Captain and the crew. Leah the Eagle even recruited several eagles to fly to St. John's to try to follow the route taken by the *Georgia K.* They all agreed to meet the next evening in Cooks Harbour, which lies on the northern tip of Newfoundland. Everyone knew they had to find the ship soon before the ice floes came down from Greenland for the winter and held it in their frozen grasp. The pressure from the ice could snap a vessel in two. Time was of the essence.

Sadly, Leah's friends had nothing to report the next evening when everyone gathered.

Leah said, "The ship must have really been blown off course. We are going to have to broaden the search."

This meant the search party would head across the Strait of Belle Isle to Labrador and search some of the outer islands. But how would they ever be able to cover all that territory?

As Toni, Leah and Glow-ria were trying to come up with a new plan suddenly the water in front of them became rocky and rough. This startled the three friends. And then, shooting up from the depths of the ocean and surfacing before them were two big beluga whales with a narwhale right behind them. Out of fear that she would be supper, Toni the Trout swam into the smallest tidal pool she could find and did not move a muscle. But the whales did not seem to be hunting. They were laughing and shouting back and forth and just seemed to be having a whale of a time. They finally noticed their audience and came to stop in front of them.

"Hello Glow-ria! Whatever are you doing here and who have you got with you? Looks like you brought us supper. Is that a nice big trout over there?" asked one of the whales.

"No, that trout is not for you and don't you get any closer to it. Now Wavie and Wilma let me introduce you to everyone."

And so the eagle and the trout, who still kept her distance, met Wavie and Wilma, the twin beluga whales, and their friend, Nora the Narwhale.

Glow-ria told the whales about Captain Woody and the *Georgia K* being lost and how it was thought that perhaps Santana, the evil wicked sea imp, was involved. All three whales offered to join in the search.

"We can cover a lot more water at a faster pace than a trout can," remarked Wilma.

"And what exactly are you trying to say?" quipped Toni.

Glow-ria stepped in before a real ruckus started. "I am sure Wilma meant nothing mean by that remark. After all, Toni, they are faster. But then again, you can get into tighter spots that they can not. Everyone has a special quality. No one is any better than the other one. We need to pull together in order to find the Captain and his crew."

Nora the Narwhale piped in, "Let's go find the Captain! And I personally would like to find the evil Santana and destroy him. I have had a few nasty run-ins with him. In fact, he's the reason I have to wear these glasses. He is also the reason I have a tusk. You see, only male narwhales are supposed have these. But Santana and a couple of nasty squid that he hangs around with came to one of our sea urchin bingo games. When someone had their slate almost filled, the squids would stretch out a tentacle and knock a sea urchin

or two off the slate. The squid would apologize and assure us it would not happen again. Well it did happen, several more times and Santana would always end up winning the game. I decided to confront them and as soon as I opened my mouth, they bolted for open waters. I chased after them and had cornered one of the squids, but the wicked creature squirted burning ink into my eyes and got away. That made me angry, so I continued to pursue one of the slimy squids. Just when I had one of them cornered, Santana jumped in front of me and shouted some strange words that turned out to be a curse. The next thing I knew, I had a giant tusk growing from my snout. Not only does this tusk get in the way, but some of the other whales make fun of me. Wavie and Wilma don't though. Anyway, that Santana needs to be taught a lesson once and for all."

Without wasting any more time, the search party, along with their new recruits, set out at once in search of the *Georgia K.*

7 Rescued

Captain Woody and Charlie, his first mate, finished dividing up the food to give to the crew. They knew they only had enough rations to last a few more days. Everyone ate their meal in silence, for the future was looking as dark as the starless foggy night.

Several deck hands cleared the dishes while Charlie went below to his cabin to retrieve his accordion. He thought that music might just soothe the crew's weary souls. He had just begun to play when a shout came from the deck above. Everyone scurried up to see what was happening. The sky that had been black and dreary was awash with light. There hovering above them was Glow-ria the Northern Light. A sense of relief filled everyone's hearts.

"We found you! We found you!" Leah screeched as she dove out of the sky and perched on the rail of the ship. "We finally found you!"

The Captain grabbed the eagle and hugged her tightly. Looking over the rail, he noticed the trout and her huge companions in the water below.

"We never thought we would be rescued. So good to see you all! Toni, who's out there with you?"

After Toni the Trout introduced the whales, Glow-ria said, "Captain Woody, what happened to you? I get a sneaky suspicion that Santana had something to do with this. Am I right?"

After Captain Woody told them what had happened, he laughed. "That Santana made a big mistake. He said we would not be found by mankind. He forgot to include my wonderful animal friends and you, Glow-ria, in his curse. I don't know what we would all have done if you hadn't found us."

The crew also thanked the rescue party.

"Now Captain," said Glow-ria, "it is not over yet. We still need to get you home. Everyone must rest for the night, for we are all weary. Tomorrow we can figure out how to get the *Georgia K* home."

Charlie, who still had the accordion in his hands, started to play a lively tune. The cook joined in on the spoons. Soon all the crewmembers were dancing on deck as Glow-ria shimmered and shook in the sky. Wavie and Wilma rose up as high as they could out of the water and twirled around until dizziness overtook them. Nora kept time to the music with her tusk. Toni even flicked her tail back and forth a few times.

The celebration continued until Captain Woody called a halt to it. "We must all get some rest. We still have a long journey ahead of us. I for one will sleep better than I have for a long time."

So Glow-ria dimmed her lights and went off to sleep wherever northern lights go to sleep. She promised to return the next evening once it was dark. Leah snuggled into a coil of rope on deck. Toni found a nice bed of kelp and snuggled in, while the whales were rocked to sleep by the gentle waves.

The next morning everyone awoke refreshed and ready to head home.

Leah the Eagle picked up the rope with her talons and took one end out to Wavie, Wilma and Nora, while the Captain secured the other to the *Georgia K*. The three whales pulled with all their might as they tried to drag the ship across the sand and back into the water.

"Wait!" cried Captain Woody. "We don't want to pull the boat into deep water without first seeing what kind of damage has been done to the underside. We don't want the vessel to sink."

"I can look at it, Captain. I need but a few inches of water. Let me try," Toni suggested. At that moment, she realized that she was just as important as a big whale. Glow-ria had been right.

The whales tugged a little more until the *Georgia K* was in the water.

Toni then disappeared to do her job. It wasn't long before she resurfaced. "Oh Captain, it is terrible. The whole keel is ripped open. There is no way this ship will stay afloat. The *Georgia K* needs major repairs."

The crew groaned in despair. Their hopes of getting home seemed crushed again. They all looked to Captain Woody for an answer.

Captain Woody paced back and forth along the deck. He stopped suddenly mid-stride. "I've got it! You animals and mammals found us and broke the curse. I bet the curse has been released off the lifeboats as well. Unfortunately, we will not be able to haul all the cargo back with us to Woody Point, but everyone can carry one package. I think if these whales make a big enough wave, the ship will be pushed back up on the beach.

That will keep it from being washed out to sea and sunk if a big storm comes up. I promise you men that we will come back and save our ship. We will not leave the *Georgia K* to rot. And we will even get home quicker, if these three beautiful whales will pull us."

The whales giggled and blushed at being called beautiful and said they would be honoured to escort the men home. With that, a loud cheer went up among the crew. Then, the Captain and Charlie started issuing orders. The crew gladly set out to perform the tasks at hand.

Rations of food and water were put into the boats and each man carried on one package. The lifeboats glided across the sand and the whales towed them out into the water. Wavie and Wilma then went back and with their mighty tails they made several magnificent waves that lifted and carried the *Georgia K* back towards the beach. When the water subsided, the ship was planted firmly on the beach. There was no danger of it being washed out to sea. The whales then returned to the boats to begin the journey home.

8 Curses, Foiled Again

The first day out in the lifeboats, Wilma, Wavie and Nora made excellent time over the calm seas. Toni managed to keep up, but by nightfall she was lagging behind. Captain Woody was concerned about his friend so he used his time to come up with a solution.

"Halt the boats!" he shouted to the whales. "I see a beach over there. Could you push us in so we can stop awhile and make a fire and have a meal?" he asked the whales.

The three whales stopped and slipped out of their harnesses. They nudged and pushed the boats as close to shore as possible so several crewmembers could jump out and haul the boats in the rest of the way. The beluga twins, along with their friend, Nora, promised to be back as soon as finished their evening meal in the depths of the sea.

Toni hung out close to the beach. Captain Woody came over with his meal and some bread. The bread he shared with the trout. He also found her some worms under a rock.

"Here you go, Toni. You must be exhausted trying to keep up with the whales. Wait right here and I will be back." The Captain strode over to the camp and after talking to the cook he came back to the beach with a big pot that he filled with seawater.

"Now Toni, may I make a suggestion? Why don't you hop in here? You will ride the rest of the way with us. It may be a little cramped, but you won't be as tired."

"You don't think anyone will make a mistake and try to cook me, do you?" Toni said while eyeing the pot suspiciously.

The Captain threw back his head and laughed. "No my dear, you will be safe in this pot. The journey would have to take a very long time before we would consider having you for supper. Not to say that a nice Bonne Bay trout such as yourself wouldn't make a fine tasty meal. But don't be so foolish. Hop in."

So Toni jumped in the pot and Captain Woody took her up to the camp. He issued an order to his crew that this brave fish was not to be disturbed.

After a couple of hours, the whales returned. The men packed up their gear and climbed back into the lifeboats. They would have to travel all night and all the next day in order to make it home before their supplies ran out. It was hard to sleep in these little boats, but some of the crewmembers found a way.

With the help of Glow-ria who had arrived at sundown, Charlie and the Captain kept watch. Glow-ria told them that Leah the Eagle was on her way to Woody Point to deliver the good news.

The next morning before daybreak, Glow-ria wished them a hardy farewell and promised to find them that evening. She was hoping that by then they would be entering the mouth of Bonne Bay heading towards Woody Point.

Later that morning, the wind picked up and the whales were struggling against the waves. To make matters worse, the fog rolled in and the boats got separated. The clever whales knew just how to remedy that problem. They talked back and forth to one another through the fog and smacked their tails on the water from time to time, so they could stay close to each other.

They had been travelling a few hours when the water in front of Captain Woody's lifeboat started churning. Suddenly Santana the evil sea imp bolted up through the surface of the water!

"Captain Woody," he hissed, "once again you have underestimated me. Did you really think you could get rid of me that easily? I see I did make one mistake when I cursed you, but I am here to end it once and for all. Nothing will save you this time."

As Santana rose up out of the water, he spotted Toni the Trout in the pot. "Oh my, fresh trout. I would so love a meal of fresh trout. Especially one that comes from Bonne Bay," he said as he snatched the pot from the Captain and

reached in. Santana grabbed the squirming, frightened trout and laughed wickedly as he held the trout up to his mouth. Just as he started to take a bite of the terrified trout, he was thrown out of the water and up into the air.

Wavie and Wilma had slipped out of their harnesses and snuck up on the evil imp. Santana, still refusing to let go of the trout was being tossed and juggled around by Wavie and Wilma.

Nora the narwhale breached, aiming her tusk at Santana. The tusk he had cursed her with. The tusk that had been made fun of. The tusk she had been ashamed of. That very tusk destroyed Santana forever. His own curse had backfired. There would be no fear of that evil wicked sea imp ever returning again.

Toni the Trout had escaped Santana's grasp at the last minute and was now back in the pot peeking out over the lip. She thanked the three whales. Years later fishermen would tell tales about the day they saw three whales and a trout frolicking in the bay.

After everyone had calmed down, the whales were again harnessed and they pulled as fast as they could towards Woody Point.

9 Back in Woody Point

Leah the Eagle soared through the air as fast as she could to get to Woody Point. As she entered the mouth of Bonne Bay, she spotted Emily and several other women standing out by the lighthouse. She came swooping down out of the sky with a loud squawk that made several of the women jump, shriek and duck. They relaxed, however, when they saw that the eagle had perched on Emily's shoulder. Everyone knew about Emily and her animal friends, but they still found it rather startling at times. Even Ann, who had been around the animals a lot more than the others were, was taken back at first.

"Leah the Eagle must have some good news. Just look at the expression on Emily's face. Come on. Let's get closer. The eagle won't hurt us." The women followed Ann over to where Emily was standing.

Emily had indeed received good news. She hugged the eagle tightly and between bursts of happy tears, told the women that the crew was on their way home. She explained why they had to leave the *Georgia K* and most of the supplies. But they were coming home, safe and sound. Nothing else mattered. With that everyone scattered to share the wonderful news and to prepare for the return of their loved ones.

Emily, with Leah still perched on her shoulder, went home. They talked some more until Emily noticed that Leah's head was nodding. "You poor dear creature, you must be exhausted. Here let me make you a nest by the fireplace. While you rest your weary wings, I will go up in to the Mystical Forest and tell the other animals. I'll be back in…" Emily stopped in mid-sentence. The eagle was already fast asleep.

Emily was walking up the hill in the Mystical Forest when she ran into Gregory A. Bear and Rhett the Fox. "Hello Emily. We heard some squawking and screeching going on and hoped it was Leah coming back with good news about Captain Woody," said the bear.

"It was news. It was wonderful news!" Emily proceeded to tell the bear and fox everything the eagle told her. When she was finished, Gregory A. Bear approached her with his arms outstretched. "It's bear hug time," he said.

Rhett, not to be outdone, bounded towards Emily. "Fox hug time, too!"

So the three friends embraced and danced around, for they could not contain their joy. When they stopped to catch their breath, Emily asked the bear and fox to go tell the moose and the caribou the wonderful news. She also asked that they all come down to her house that evening. She had a couple of ideas in mind to celebrate the homecoming of the Captain and his crew.

After a peaceful nap, Leah awoke to the smell of warm buttery toast. She so loved warm buttery toast. Following her nose, the eagle went into the kitchen. Emily smiled when she saw Leah and put a platter down on the table. Leah perched on the back of a chair. She balanced herself on one leg and grasped a piece of toast in her talons. She and Emily had a nice chat. She told the eagle about her plans for Captain Woody's return. She had a lot to do before then. *If only I knew how close Captain Woody was*, she wondered. Then she had an idea.

"I know I am asking too much, but would you fly out and see what kind of progress they are making? I just can't stand not knowing if they are still alright."

Leah the Eagle admitted she was curious too and agreed to fly out and check on the Captain and his crew. She said that she would come straight back with the news. And since it was evening, she would find them faster because of Glow-ria's guiding light. The eagle had a few more bites of toast and out the door she flew in search of the three lifeboats.

Shortly after Leah left the animals appeared on Emily's doorstep. Emily stood out on the porch telling them some of her plans to celebrate the Captain's return. When she told them that she was on her way to the lodge to meet with the townsfolk, the animals decided to join her. They couldn't go into the building, so they stood outside by a window while Emily told to them what was happening.

All at once, an unexpected snowstorm started. The people were cold because of the open window so they invited Emily's friends to join them inside the lodge. Before the meeting was over, John Lawrence the Moose, Rhett the Fox and Gregory A. Bear had become honorary members. Just imagine that group picture of the lodge members!

When the meeting ended, Emily said goodbye to her four-legged friends and headed home. She was exhausted and was looking forward to a peaceful sleep. Just as she was crawling into bed, she heard a tap on the window. Leah had returned. Emily flung open the window and the eagle came in and told her all the news about Captain Woody and the demise of Santana. It looked as if they would arrive home late tomorrow. Leah the eagle went downstairs and snuggled up in her makeshift nest by the fireplace. Emily curled back up in bed and with a smile on her face, drifted off to sleep.

The next day, Emily arose and after a quick breakfast, she went to Betty's and told her the grand news. Then the two of them walked over to Ann's and let her know that her husband should be home by nightfall. Betty and Ann went around Woody Point delivering the good news to everyone. Emily went back to her house to work on a project for her husband's return. In fact, the whole town was busy preparing for the return of the crew of the *Georgia K.*

10 A Safe Port

With no other obstacles in the way, the whales made record time as they swam past Lobster Cove Head Lighthouse. The men all cheered and could barely contain their excitement. They would soon be in Woody Point. They had made it home. They were safe. As they came around Mudge's Point they saw a wonderful magnificent sight. Boats lit up like Christmas trees were all lined up waiting for them. Above them, Glow-ria was shining brighter than all the stars that had joined her in the sky. The other boats surrounded the three lifeboats and escorted them the rest of the way to the wharf. It seemed as if the whole town had turned out to greet Captain Woody and his crew. Glow-ria's magnificent light lit up the whole wharf. Several local musicians were playing lively jigs as people danced around. Others were standing at end of wharf cheering the boats on.

Captain Woody tied off his boat and climb up over the wharf. Just when he straightened up, he found himself looking straight into Emily's eyes. He could not express how happy he was to see his loving wife. Not too long ago he had feared he would never see her again. Emily must have felt the same way as she rushed into the arms of her darling Captain. But Emily and the Captain were not alone—the whole town shared these feelings of joy, relief and excitement.

Emily wanted to reward Wavie, Wilma, Nora and Toni, so she bent down over the side of the wharf and placed a laurel on each of the beluga twin's heads. She gave Toni a bright red bow. Nora the Narwhale, who had destroyed Santana, was presented with a medallion dangling from a ribbon. Etched on the medallion was *I am a wonderful, brave and unique being.*

The whales and the trout were pleased with their gifts and after thanking Emily they danced around the bay jumping in and out of water and performing other tricks, much to the delight of the crowd. With one last flick of their tails they headed out of the bay towards open water. Wavie, Wilma and Nora escorted Toni back to her home and bid farewell to their new little friend.

The festivities soon broke up and people started heading home. The crewmembers were tired and hungry and in need of a good rest before they went back out to sea in a few days to save the *Georgia K.* The Captain looked so very tired, so Emily whistled loudly. Charlene the Caribou pulling a sleigh trotted towards them and got them quickly home. As they were getting out of the sleigh, Emily thanked her friend and then leaned in and whispered something in the caribou's ear.

"What was that whispering all about?" asked Captain Woody, as they walked arm and arm to the house.

"Oh nothing," answered Emily with a mischievous look on her face.

Later that evening Captain Woody had eaten a warm hardy meal and enjoyed a long hot bath. He had just come downstairs and was getting ready to relax in his chair by the fire, when a knock came at the door.

"I wonder who that could be at this hour?" he said as he walked towards the door.

"Well it definitely isn't thieves," giggled Emily.

Glossary

imp	small demon
impending	something that is going to happen in the near future
St. John's	capital of Newfoundland
The Narrows	name for a narrow passage of water between two cliffs, in St Johns Harbour
omen	a happening that foretells a future event
assess	to determine or estimate
bellowed	to cry out loudly
menacing	threatening harm or evil
waterspout	funnel-shaped column of air full of spray, occurring over water
issue	to put forth
meddling	to concern yourself with other people's problems and affairs
bewilderment	confusion
enlist	to get the help of someone

kelp	a type of seaweed
disgruntled	unhappy with a situation or thing
hampered	kept from moving or acting freely
essence	of the greatest importance
Strait of Belle Isle	A body of water that runs between Newfoundland and Labrador
turbulent	wild irregular motion
beluga whale	large white toothed whale of northern seas
narwhale (or narwhal)	very rare toothed whale with a long spiral tusk extending from upper jaw
tentacle	long, slender, flexible growths about the head or mouth of some animals
sea urchin	a spiny shell fish
tusk	a very long large pointed tooth that projects from the mouth
bolt	a sudden movement
alders	a small group of rapidly growing trees that are members of the birch family
foul weather gear	waterproof clothing to protect against high seas and rain
sou'wester	the hat that is part of the foul weather gear

toboggan	a long, narrow, flat sled without runners. Made of thin boards curved up in the front
Northern lights	also known as the aurora borealis. Irregular lights that can be viewed in the northern sky
Screech	to make a high pitched harsh sound
keel	the bottom of the boat
solution	the answer to a problem
Bonne Bay	(pronounced bonn) a body of water on the west coast of Newfoundland with many communities surrounding it
churning	stirring or shaking
hurtling	to be thrown or fling with force
frolicking	having fun
talons	eagle's claws
lodge	place for meetings and other social gatherings
obstacle	anything that gets in the way
jigs	fast, springy dances
medallion	a large medal
unique	to be different in thought and manner

Look for these other great
Emily & the Captain books

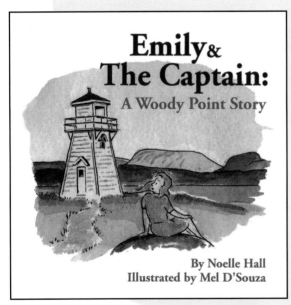

**Emily&
The Captain:**
A Woody Point Story

By Noelle Hall
Illustrated by Mel D'Souza

Emily & the Captain:
A Winter Adventure

By Noelle Hall
Illustrated by Mel D'Souza

ISBN 0-9685004-2-0 $6.50 US $9.95 CAN   ISBN 0-9685004-8-X $6.50 US $9.95 CAN

About the Author

Noelle Chason Hall, a daughter of a Newfoundlander and an American serviceman, has spent many of her summers, since childhood, in Woody Point, Bonne Bay on the west coast of Newfoundland. Her books reflect the love she has for the area. She later attended Memorial University of Newfoundland. A member of the Virginia State Reading in Education Association, Noelle is an avid promoter of literacy in the United States and Canada and spends as much time as possible visiting schools and raising funds for libraries. Although her first love is writing, Noelle also assists in museum operations and with planning special events for Ferry Farm, George Washington's Boyhood Home, in Stafford, Virginia. Her pet project is the annual *Read, By George* literary event. She is also a Realtor for Keller Williams Real Estate. The author lives in Spotsylvania, Virginia, with her husband, Gregory, but spends as much time as she can at her house in Woody Point, Newfoundland, which she affectionately calls her "little cocoon."

About the Illustrator

Mel D'Souza is an illustrator and cartoonist for *Downhome Magazine*. Mel lives in Brampton, Ontario but travels frequently and extensively across Newfoundland and Labrador. He also has his summer home in Francois on the Southwest coast of Newfoundland. Mel's ability to capture the essence of a story in pictures is reflected in the delightful sketches that illustrate this book.